T0418491

Wave Warrior

Lesley Choyce

orca soundings

ORCA BOOK PUBLISHERS

For all my fellow Nova Scotian surfers. —LC

Library and Archives Canada Cataloguing in Publication

Choyce, Lesley, 1951-
Wave warrior / Lesley Choyce.
(Orca soundings)

ISBN 978-1-55143-649-4 (bound) ISBN 978-1-55143-647-0 (pbk.)

1. Surfing--Juvenile fiction. I. Title. II. Series.
PS8555.H668W29 2007 JC813'.54 C2006-907055-5

First published in the United States, 2007
Library of Congress Control Number: 2006940638

Summary: Ben wants to learn to surf but he is terrified. When he meets an aging surfer, Ben learns the way of the wave warrior.

MIX
Paper from
responsible sources
FSC® C016245

Orca Book Publishers is dedicated to preserving the environment and has printed this book on paper certified by the Forest Stewardship Council.®

Orca Book Publishers gratefully acknowledges the support for its publishing programs provided by the following agencies: the Government of Canada through the Canada Book Fund and the Canada Council for the Arts, and the Province of British Columbia through the BC Arts Council and the Book Publishing Tax Credit.

Cover photography by Dreamstime

ORCA BOOK PUBLISHERS
PO Box 5626, Stn. B
Victoria, BC Canada
V8R 6S4

ORCA BOOK PUBLISHERS
PO Box 468
Custer, WA USA
98240-0468

www.orcabook.com
Printed and bound in Canada.

14 13 12 11 • 6 5 4 3

To live with fear and not be afraid is the final test of maturity.   —Edward Weeks

Chapter One

All my life, surfers had been coming to my beach—Lawrencetown Beach in Nova Scotia. There were tall surfers, short surfers, skinny surfers and fat surfers. Hairy surfers and shaved-head surfers. Smart surfers and stupid surfers. Surfers with great cars. Surfers who hitchhiked. Surfers who were friendly and surfers who were rude and nasty. There were even girl surfers who sometimes smiled at me.

Even though I lived by the ocean, I had never surfed. I was a lousy swimmer, and I knew the sea could be dangerous. There were rip currents near the headland that pulled swimmers so far out to sea that helicopters had to save them or pick up whatever was left. And sometimes there were huge killer waves.

It was a dangerous world out there once you left dry land. My grandfather— a great old guy—had been a fisherman.

"Ben," my grandfather told me one day while we were watching some kids from the city surf overhead waves, "you don't play around with the North Atlantic Ocean. I used to risk my life to go out there and catch a couple of darn fish so we didn't starve. But you don't just go out there in that friggin' cold water for the fun of it." He had died last spring, and I still missed him.

His words stuck with me. He was right. It could be dangerous. People had drowned at Lawrencetown, unaware of how treacherous it could be. And it *was* bloody cold, even in the summer. Surfers had to wear wet suits almost all the time. There were a few warm days when people came out from Halifax and swam in their bathing suits, but they were rare. Usually the water was so cold it was painful. Maybe I was smart to avoid the ocean.

But it was driving me crazy. Despite everything my grandfather said, despite every reason there was to avoid it, I wanted to surf so bad it was ripping a hole in my head. I had to at least try.

My parents were opposed to it.

"I'm sixteen," I told them. "I can decide for myself."

"You remember what your grandfather told you," my father said. He had not become a fisherman like his father but worked at a place in Burnside that made cardboard boxes.

"You're going to get hurt, I know it," my mom said. "What if you drown?"

"I'm not going to drown. I'll have a wet suit on. It will keep me afloat."

"You're going to put your body in one of those rubber things?" my dad asked. "I'd rather eat nails with ketchup."

"I'm going surfing," I said. And left, slamming the door.

Chapter Two

It was a sunny Saturday in the middle of June. Goofy's surf truck was parked by the rocks that acted as a seawall to keep the ocean from washing out the road. Goofy rented boards and wet suits to anyone silly enough to brave the early summer sea that was just a few degrees above zero. It didn't look cold but it was.

I paid the money and went behind the rocks to put on the wet suit. It felt tight and weird. Goofy, smiling that idiotic smile that gave him his name, had also rented me a six-foot "fish"—a shortboard with a *V* in the tail and four short fins. It was the board I'd seen the hot surfers use to really rip.

I was gonna be like them—on my first day. If I could only stop my heart from racing so fast and my knees from shaking.

I watched a few experienced surfers paddle out. The waves were shoulder high, not small, but not too big. I wrapped the strap of the leash around my ankle, took a deep breath and waded into the ocean. I had on boots, but without gloves the cold water knifed into my hands. I tried to lie on the board and paddle like I'd seen the others do. In no time I slipped off and went right under. Talk about a wake-up call. A voice screamed inside my head. I surfaced and gasped for air. I knew it was going to be cold, but not that cold.

I was still in the shallows, ready to quit and run home to momma. I faced the shore. Then I heard someone behind me let out a loud whoop. I turned to watch Gorbie Kessler riding a beautiful blue wall of water. He kicked his board high up into the wave, made a radical turn and fell off face-first into the water. When he came up he was laughing.

I pointed my board away from the beach. I lay on it. I wobbled. I paddled. A wave came at me and I paddled into it, tucked my head down and then I was over it. I kept paddling straight out to sea. I didn't even look up until I was near where the other surfers were sitting close to the takeoff zone. I was breathing hard. Man, was I out of shape.

"Yo, Ben." It was Weed. You can guess why he was named that. "Thought you didn't surf."

Still gasping for breath and trying to sit up on my board, I said, "Times change." Or not.

"Just go for it," he said, laughing. Nothing bothered Weed. He probably didn't even feel the cold. I watched as he paddled and caught a nice little waist-high wave. It looked like there was nothing to it.

I missed the first seven waves. I flailed and thrashed my arms. I dug deep and paddled. But I couldn't get it. I'd been in the water about forty-five minutes when I heard someone yell, "Outside!" I'd been around enough to know that this meant there was a wave coming that was bigger than the rest. I turned. Yeah, it looked like a killer to me. I didn't know what to do, but the lunatic who resides in the back of my brain repeated what Weed had said. Just go for it.

So I went for it.

And got eaten for lunch.

It went like this. I paddled toward shore with all my strength. I felt the wave catch up to me and begin to lift me into the sky. I was holding onto the rails of my board for dear life. I was moving faster than I could imagine. But it all happened so quickly. I was dropping down the face of a steep wall of ocean.

My mouth was open. I know that because when I did the face-plant into the bottom of the wave, I was gargling salt water, thinking that maybe I was about to die. The wave drove me deep into the water. I flapped my arms around, thinking that going back up to the surface was a good idea.

But it wasn't. At least not then.

I surfaced just in time to open my eyes and see my airborne surfboard eclipsing the morning sun. And aimed straight for my head. *Wham*.

The next thing I knew I had this awful pain from where the board had slammed onto the bridge of my nose. The fin had connected just below my eye. And there was blood.

Blood and pain and floundering around in cold water with another wave about to break on you. This is not a great combination.

Weed saw what happened. "Man, you got nailed. Better get to shore."

I didn't know which way shore was.

"That way, Ben. You okay?"

Okay was not the word I would use. But I was alive. I nodded and tasted blood. At least I hadn't been blinded. I dog-paddled to shore, my board in tow.

I swore I would never, ever, do that again.

Chapter Three

My mother wanted to take me to the hospital, but I said no way. She could see how I was feeling and tried to be nice. When my dad came home he slammed into the told-you-so lectures. I loved my father, but he could be a pain in the butt sometimes. I finally told him to go to hell and stormed out of the house.

I biked to the headland and sat high above the sea, facing west. The sun was going down and the sky was beautiful. Below, at the mouth of the river, some guys were surfing. I knew all about the river current here that could pull swimmers out to sea. But tonight, the tide was high and there was no danger of that. From here it all looked so graceful, so easy. I was jealous of the surfers, and I hated myself for being such a loser. And then Tara appeared, walking up the headland toward me.

I touched my nose and it hurt. I knew Tara surfed. I'd watched her putting on her wet suit in the parking lot. I'd seen her grab her board, run across the sand to the ocean and paddle out. She was new at it but she could ride waves. She was also beautiful with her curly brown hair, freckles and funny T-shirts. It seemed odd that she was always alone when she arrived, and she kept to herself. Not once had I gotten up the nerve to even say hi to her on the beach. I sure as heck didn't want to talk to her now. But I sat there frozen.

I just stared out to sea, hoping she'd walk on by. But it wasn't going to work out that way.

I knew she had stopped but I didn't turn.

"Ouch," she said. "How'd that happen?"

I took a breath and half turned toward her. "A wipeout. I got nailed by the board." I didn't tell her it was only my first wave, my first real attempt at surfing.

She knelt down beside me. "It got you on the nose?"

"Yeah."

"And the black eye?"

I didn't know I had a black eye. I didn't know that was the way it happened. Get socked in the nose hard enough and a while later you have a black eye. "Oh great," I said.

"Does it hurt?"

"Yes."

"Waves can be brutal."

So can life, I wanted to say. "How do they do it?" I asked, pointing to the surfers below.

Tara was now sitting on the grass with me. Our feet were dangling over the edge of the cliff. The sky was on fire as the sun began to set. At least when it was dark no one would notice the black eye.

"No one just gets in the water, catches waves and rides. It takes a lot of practice. A lot of wipeouts."

"Can you imagine what I would look like by my third day of trying to learn?"

Tara laughed. "When people ask about your eye, don't tell them. Let them make up their own stories. It'll be much more interesting that way. Let me look." Then she leaned toward me. I could smell the sweetness of her and

I felt paralyzed. She was looking right into my eyes. "That's amazing," she said.

"What is?" I asked.

"By tomorrow morning, you're gonna look like you had a fistfight with a gorilla."

"And lost."

"Gonna try it again?"

"No way," I said.

"I'll teach you."

I don't know why I did what I did next. I guess it was my pride. And I was sure she was just feeling sorry for me.

"Yeah, right," I said sarcastically.

"What?" I could tell I'd hurt her feelings. Now I knew just how big of an idiot and loser I really was. I couldn't bring myself to say anything else.

I got on my bike and rode the grassy path back to the road. It was the beginning of summer and already I was wishing it was over.

The next day was Sunday. At break-fast my mom stared at me. "You sure we shouldn't go to the hospital? What if your nose is broken?"

"It's not broken. Besides, I'm not going to wait around for hours in an emergency room all day."

"He's right," my father added, oddly coming to my defense. "Besides, it's no big deal. I've had worse than that. It builds character." He was smiling. I think he was secretly proud of me. A black eye meant I was becoming a man. I could take the punishment.

"I'll be okay," I said. "I just feel like hiding for a while."

"You can't hide, Ben," my mom said. "It's summer. You need fresh air."

My father cleared his throat. "Well, I was talking to my boss about getting you a summer job in the plant."

Working in a factory that made cardboard boxes sounded like a death sentence. I knew that anything I said now would be the wrong thing. Luckily, my mother agreed with me. "I don't think Ben should do that." She paused and looked at me. "He's still a boy. He shouldn't have to grow up yet."

"When I was his age…" my father began, but he was cut off by my mother.

"We all know about what you did when you were his age, dear."

That was the end of that conversation. The job at the box factory would hang over my head all summer unless I found something to do that would keep me out of the house. And I wasn't sure my mother's small victory was going to save me altogether. My old man would keep alive his dream of getting his son a job at his factory. And if he had his way, that would be the end of my so-called life.

Chapter Four

I wasn't sure why I kept going back
to watch the surfers. I would sit on
the rocks and watch Genghis, Gorbie,
Weed, Tim and all the others arrive in
their cars with music blasting. Then
they changed into their wet suits,
sometimes stripping naked and not
caring who saw.

I watched wannabe surfers renting boards from Goofy at his surf truck and paddling out into the shore break. By one o'clock on a weekend afternoon, the beach would be crowded. Everything out here had changed. When I was little and my mom and I walked on the beach, it was almost always empty. Maybe one or two old-guy surfers. But nothing like this.

Tara was there too. She looked at me, but I avoided her. She'd probably never bother to try to talk to me again.

Goofy was between rentals when he yelled to me. "Benji Boy, c'mere."

I walked over. He had that big goofy grin on his face. He smelled like he'd been toking up.

"Benji, you paid for a day and used the board for maybe thirty minutes. Why don't you give it another go?"

"Duh," I said, pointing at my face.

"Salt water would do it good. Fall off a horse, you gotta get back on."

"Thanks, Goof, but no way."

I watched as Tara picked up her board and ran for the water. She looked as if she couldn't wait to get out there and surf. Part of me still felt the same way. But the horse had knocked me off and then kicked me hard. I was afraid to try again.

I turned to walk home and saw this old dog. And I mean old—graying hair, ancient filmy eyes and droopy jowls. I stooped and petted him. It seemed to take all the effort he could muster to wag his tail. I glanced around and it didn't look like he belonged to anyone.

"Whose dog are you?" I asked.

More tail wagging.

"Lost?"

Those sad eyes again. But he began to walk, and then he stopped and looked back at me like he wanted me to follow. I followed.

The dog trotted slowly off to the empty end of the beach, where he stopped by an old Ford camper van. The van had California plates and four longboards strapped to the racks on the roof. The license plate read *Surf's Up* and the side doors were open. Inside, an old guy was napping on the bed. The dog began to lap from a steel water bowl.

"California dog, eh?" I said to my slobbering friend.

The man inside stirred and then suddenly sat bolt upright. He glared at me. "You trying to steal my dog?" he snapped.

"What?"

"Mickey D there. You weren't thinking about stealing him and selling him for medical research?"

"What are you, crazy?"

He laughed. "You better believe I'm crazy. I've got scars to prove it and three ex-wives that would testify on my behalf." He got out of the van, moving quickly as if he was just a kid. But he was old. "I was only joking. Mickey D finds people and brings them to me."

"Mickey D's the dog, right?"

"Yeah. Named for Mickey Dora. Surfer I once knew. You surf, kid?"

His eyes were blue and they seemed to penetrate deep into me. His skin was tanned like old leather and he had a scraggly beard of gray and a head of thinning blond-gray hair. The Hawaiian shirt, cutoff jeans and leather sandals completed the picture.

"Tried," I said. "Tried and failed."

He stared at my face. "Oh, I see. Heck, I thought that was a tattoo. Where I come from, people pay to have something hideous like that put on their face."

"California, right?"

"What are you, a boy genius? You go to Harvard or what?"

He made me laugh. Crazy or not, I liked this guy.

"School's out, so I'm giving my brain cells a rest."

"At least you have brain cells. And they still work. You're in good shape by my estimates." He stuck out his hand. "Ray," he said. "Ray Cluny, from Santa Barbara."

"Ben Currie, from Lawrencetown Beach."

We shook hands, and I thought he was going to rip my arm off.

"Freaking Nova Scotia," Ray said, staring up toward the sun. "I've been wanting to get here for years. Always wimped out at the drive. It's a long way from the Pacific. But I'm here now. Figured it was now or never."

"How long are you here for?"

"As long as it takes," he said mysteriously. "They said it would be like going back in time. Like California in the early sixties. Before the Beach Boys. Before all that."

I was trying to calculate how old he must be but couldn't do the math. "You've been surfing a long time?"

"Sixty years. Maybe more."

"Holy mackerel. How old are you?"

"Seventy-five and thanks for asking, kid. It makes me feel right young to have to say it out loud. Look at Mickey D there. In dog years, he's a hundred."

Mickey D had curled up and lay by the tire. His eyes were closed. He looked content.

"What brought you here?"

"Where I live, you can't get a wave on your own. Everywhere is crowded now. Not like the old days. Surfing is all hyped up and commercialized. You can't get away from it. But here, you still have elbow room. A guy could have a clean wave all to himself. Have some fun. Like the old days. You know any good breaks? Secret spots, that sort of thing."

"Yeah, I do," I said slowly.

Ray thought my pause meant something else. "But you're keeping them to yourself, right? I can dig it."

"No, it wasn't that. I could take you there. Down past Three Fathom Harbor. Near where my grandfather had his fish shack."

"Like the old man and the sea. Bet your granddad has some stories."

"*Had* stories. He died not long ago."

"Sorry. It hurts, doesn't it, when someone close to you dies?"

"Yeah, it hurts." And I suddenly realized that thinking about my grandfather made me feel like I was about to cry. Ray could tell.

"Sorry. I blurt things out. I'll try not to do it again. Got a board and wet suit? Wanna share some of that shore break on the other side of the dune with all those hotshots and an old kahuna?"

I shook my head no. "No board. No wet suit. And I'm still recovering from my first surf lesson."

Ray smiled broadly. "I got extra boards and wet suits. What do you say?"

I looked at the other cars in the parking lot. There would be a dozen or more kids in the shore break. I couldn't handle them laughing at me as I struggled to learn.

"I can't," I said. "Not here. Not now. I'll watch you from the beach."

Ray smiled again. "Okay," he said with a mock-threatening look on his face.

"But it's not over. Your time will come. Mickey D will track you down and drag you back here, Ben. And I'm going to get you to show me that secret break, even if I have to bribe you."

I walked off down the beach. I thought I was headed home, but I came back twenty minutes later and saw Mickey D sitting by the edge of the water. Ray was out there on his longboard—one old guy of seventy-five and a bunch of young surfers on tiny boards. He was catching more waves than any of them, and he was cruising across those long blue walls of water like some kind of Hawaiian surf god.

And part of me was thinking, I'm never going to be able to do that. Not in a million years.

Chapter Five

It rained for almost a week after that. If it wasn't raining, the fog was so thick you couldn't see your hand in front of your face. There was nothing for me to do but hang around the house, watch bad TV reruns and get bored.

By Thursday, my mom was siding with my father. "Ben, maybe you'd be better off working with your father than just moping around the house."

"I'm not moping," I lied. I was hiding out from the world until I looked half normal. The black had turned to blue and I hoped it was fading. I kept thinking about Tara. And about surfing. And about the fact that my life was over before I even got my ass out of high school. I ate a lot. Pretty soon I'd be fat as well.

While flipping through the satellite channels, I discovered the sports network had a documentary about old guys who surfed. It was way cool. These were the legendary surfers, now all over sixty, who had surfed the big North Shore waves of Hawaii back in the early 1960s. They showed them at Waimea and Sunset and then shifted to years later when they were surfing in the crowds in California. Some were bald, some had big guts, some were skinny and had a crazed look in their eyes.

And then there was Ray. I didn't believe it at first. I watched him being interviewed. "Guess we can rightfully call you a kahuna now," the young interviewer said.

"Guess you can," Ray said and laughed. It was unmistakably him. They ran some old black-and-white footage of him in 1962 at Malibu. He was smooth as ice. Next it was back to the older Ray surfing a big wave in Northern California. He was on that board I'd seen him ride. He was amazing.

"Any advice to young surfers?" the interviewer asked over the video clip.

"Fight your inner demons," Ray said. "Be a warrior. Don't ever let the suckers get to you."

And then they cut to a commercial for SUVs.

The rain was still pelting down, but I put on my father's serious rain gear and headed out. I walked to the beach and heard the roar of the storm waves. The beach parking lot was empty—all except for the van with California plates. I banged on the side door and the dog barked.

When the door opened, Ray saw me standing there. "What's a kahuna?" I blurted out.

Ray laughed. "You've been watching too much TV. It rots your mind. Wanna come in out of the rain or do you prefer to drown in it?" He coughed long and hard as I stepped up and inside. I found myself settling into a swivel captain's chair on the front driver's side.

"A kahuna is what they call you when you're old. When you're young and stupid, you're a gremmie or a grem or a grommet. When you're old,

you're a kahuna, or if they don't like
you, you're a kook. As long as you're not
a poser you're okay."

"Poser?"

"Someone who hangs around surf,
talks the talk, walks the walk, but
doesn't surf."

"Oh."

"What? You, a poser? No way. You
got the beauty mark to prove it."

"But I can't surf." I leaned over and
petted Mickey D, who was already
asleep and snoring on the floor.

Ray coughed again. He closed the
door as the rain began to blow in.

"I want you to teach me to surf,"
I said quickly.

Ray said nothing. He reached above
his head and pulled down an old *Surfer*
magazine. He flipped it to a two-page
spread of a surfer, somewhat out of focus,
surfing one of the biggest waves I'd ever
seen. I read the caption and got the picture.

"I'm not only gonna teach you to surf, kid. I'm gonna teach you to be a wave warrior."

"Sounds violent."

"Not violent, dude. It's a whole different kind of battle."

I stared at the huge wave again—triple overhead with a threatening lip. "You made it, right?"

Ray shook his head. "Nope. Two seconds after a buddy of mine took that picture I was pearling up to my waist. I got sucked down, chewed up, pulled up to the top and thrown back down under. I got the air knocked out of me, had my arms and legs nearly pulled from their sockets and thought I saw angels in bikinis."

"Were you scared?"

"No, Ben," he said sarcastically, "I was feeling just fine. Hell, yes, I was scared. I figured I was about to die."

"What saved you?"

He closed the magazine and put it back on the shelf. He grinned crazily. "I had this vision, see. It was my grandmother. Yep, right there beneath three thousand million gallons of Pacific Ocean. She spoke to me just as I was about to struggle to get to the surface. 'Relax,' she said. 'If you want to live, you can't struggle. Let yourself sink.' Well, that seemed like the last thing I wanted to do. I wanted air and I wanted it badly."

"But you listened?"

"Son, when your dead grandmother appears to you after the worst wipeout of your life and tells you what to do, you better take the advice."

"I would have quit after that."

"I did. For two weeks. But it didn't take. I just decided to ride ten-foot waves instead of forty-foot waves. My close encounter with the hereafter gave me a new appreciation of life."

"So now you're a kahuna?"

"No, man. Now I'm an old kook with an old dog and a bunch of old boards. And I came here to Nova Scotia to..." He stopped himself and looked away.

"To what?"

Ray coughed. "To teach a chubby kid with a black eye how to catch a wave and stand up."

"When?"

"Whenever the rain stops."

Chapter Six

The rain stopped on Saturday night. Sunday was golden. I was up early and rode my bike to the beach without eating anything. It was only eight o'clock but there were already dozens of cars in the parking lot, mostly surfers. This was not good. I wasn't going to attempt surfing in front of city surfers who already knew what they were doing.

I didn't see Ray's van anywhere. And there was Tara, taking her board down from the top of her friend's car. She already had her wet suit on and she looked stunning. I guess I was staring at her when she turned around. She said nothing.

"Hi," I said nervously. "Good waves?"

"Awesome," she said. "Shoulder high. Glassy. You gonna surf?"

"Dunno," I answered. "Have a good one."

I turned around and decided that, for sure, I should go home. I was ready to handle the pain of whatever wipeout was coming my way, but not the humiliation of Tara and the others watching me.

I was pedaling slowly out of the parking lot, thinking, no Ray, no way. So I was off the hook.

But just then Ray's van swung into the beach lot and drove straight at me.

It stopped inches from my front wheel. Ray leaned out. "Ben, I'm stoked. What a swell. Get in. You're gonna show me that secret spot you were talking about."

"I don't think…" I began.

"That's right, gremlin, don't think. There's no time for thinking. This is what I came to Nova Scotia for. I've been down the coast a few miles. I can see the possibilities, but I bet you can steer me to the right spot. The beach here is gonna be too crowded for me. Put your damn bike on my rack on the back of the van."

So I strapped my bike on the back and got in.

"You're riding shotgun now, partner. Just point me to surfing paradise."

"East," I said.

"East it is."

Not far past Three Fathom Harbor is the roadway to an old broken-down farmhouse and barn. You could drive down there and park, and if you walked a ways up onto the eroded headland, you could see the waves. But unless you were right there, you wouldn't think it was a good surf spot. No one surfed there and you couldn't see it from the road. I took Ray there. My grandfather had first brought me here when I was a kid to watch for whales on a warm summer day. Now it was my turn to share this place with Ray.

He stood speechless.

"It's a point break," I said. "A left."

"It's flawless," Ray said. "What do you call this place?"

"I just call it the Farm."

"A bit dull for a name, don't you think?" he said. "It needs something better than that."

"Right."

"Now we surf. Lesson number one."

Mickey D sat down on his haunches at the top of the headland and looked out to sea as Ray and I ran back to his van. Yeah, I had to run to keep up with a seventy-five-year-old dude from California.

Ray tossed me a wet suit and some boots. "It'll be a little tight. You tuck that baby fat in there and it'll work. And remember, you can't sink with it on. Neoprene will float you. Trust it."

I was both excited and nervous. The suit felt really weird. "Ray, I don't know the first thing about surfing. I only tried that once."

"You only need to know one thing. You can do this. It may not be pretty, but you can do this."

We were walking across the old pasture, full wet suits on, longboards under our arms. The sun beating down and no wind at all. Mickey D watched from above as we scrambled over the big rocks by the shoreline and began to paddle out.

"This is perfect," Ray told me. "We follow this deep channel out to the point. Won't even get our hair wet."

I was lying down, paddling hard and slipping sideways, not able to stay centered or balanced. When I slipped off, Ray would stop paddling and wait.

"Good plan, Ben. Get a little water in the suit. Get the juices of the old Atlantic swirling around. How's it feel?"

"Like ice."

"Cold, huh? Who'd think the sea would be so cold here the first weekend of July?"

I climbed back onto my board.

"Wave warriors never mind the cold," he said.

What was with this wave warrior thing? All I wanted was to get through the day without dying.

When we reached the takeoff zone directly in front of the point, Ray said nothing. He faced the shoreline, paddled deep, caught a smooth five-foot wall of water and dropped down the face of it like it was the easiest thing in the world. And he was gone. I tried sitting up on my board but fell off again into the icy water. Four waves passed under me as I got back on my board. The leash kept it from floating away. God bless the man who invented surf leashes.

When Ray returned, he looked ten years younger. "The Farm, eh? I rename this Nirvana Farm."

"Like the band?"

"Nah. Like where the Buddhists go when they die for good. Now it's your turn. Get your board headed straight for shore."

Easier said than done, but after falling off two more times I had the headland staring straight at me.

"Lie down with the nose of the board just slightly out of the water."

I was breathing hard. And I was shaking.

"Good. Now here comes a set. Let the first three pass under you."

I felt the swells move under me, but I stayed put.

"Now for this next one, paddle like your life depends on it."

So I paddled as hard as I could and I was shocked. The wave suddenly grew steep, real steep. I had actually caught the wave, but my board was rocketing straight for the bottom. I realized that I'd been here before. Then *wham*.

I did a full frontal face-plant in the trough of the wave and lost the board. Water was forced up my nostrils, and in a split second I was under water, getting pummeled like a mouse in a washing machine.

Then it was over. I'd swallowed some water, but I popped up. The wave had passed and my board floated nearby.

Another wave was coming at me. "Get away from your board," Ray yelled. "Dive."

So I dove and I felt the last wave of the set rumble over top of me. When I surfaced, the board was still nearby. And I was still alive.

Chapter Seven

Ray kept an eye on me as I struggled to paddle back to the lineup after each attempt to catch a wave. I racked up ten wipeouts.

"You're doing just fine. You can catch the waves. All you have to do is keep the nose from pearling."

"Pearling?"

"Digging in. Lean back once you've caught the wave."

On the next wave, I leaned back and, well, I wiped out, but not right away. I actually dropped down the face, and then I skidded out in front of the wave. I was so excited I tried to stand up. That's when I slipped off the board and got walloped by the wall of water behind me. I came up spitting sea juice. But I was smiling.

I never did stand up that day. And I was waterlogged. But it felt good.

Ray suddenly looked tired. "Ready to go ashore?" he asked.

"Yeah. I'm stoked but wasted."

"It's a good combination."

I looked up at the headland just then and there was a girl sitting with Mickey D. I squinted into the sun to get a good look. It was Tara. And she saw me looking. I waved to her, but she didn't wave back. Instead, she stood up and clapped her hands as if she had just watched a performance of some kind— my performance.

Mickey D met us on the beach, wagging his tail but having a hard time walking on the slippery rocks. Tara was nowhere in sight. Ray had to sit down before we walked the long hike back to his van. "I'm out of shape, dude. Too much driving. Too much time cramped up in the van." Ray looked a little pale just then.

"You all right?"

"All right is relative, Ben. I'm not as good as I used to be. But I'm not dead yet." He laughed and coughed so hard I was afraid he'd hurt himself.

"Wanna stay at my house for a bit? You'd get to sleep in a bed."

"I'm not a mooch. I don't think I'd be comfortable at your ole homestead.

Rather be in the van. Stay close to the water."

"You want to be close to the water?"

"Yeah. I need to be able to wake up, look out the window and see the ocean."

"I got an idea," I said.

After we wrestled ourselves out of the wet suits, I told Ray I wanted to take him on a sightseeing tour.

"Food first," he said, and he set out a loaf of whole wheat bread, a jar of peanut butter and one of homemade jelly. Ray made a big sandwich for me, one for Mickey D and one for himself. There was so much peanut butter in it that the whole thing stuck to the roof of my mouth and I could hardly swallow. Mickey D wolfed his down in four bites. So did Ray. "Where to?" Ray asked, picking up his keys.

We drove out to the fishermen's shacks at the end of Osprey Island Road, and I told him to stop in front of an old weathered three-room structure by the harbor there. "It was my grandfather's," I said. "He didn't live here, but he stayed here overnight if he was going out to sea in the morning."

I led Ray first out onto the rickety wooden wharf that was attached. He was wide-eyed as he looked into the deep clear water. "Your granddad was a fisherman?"

"Up until the time the fish were gone."

"Damn."

"Come on in." I found the key under an old fish crate by the window and opened the door. "You can stay here if you like. No one's been using the place since he died." I felt like crying. Ray could see it in my face.

"I love it," Ray said, looking out the window at the sparkling water just a few feet from the shack. "I'd like to call it home for a while." Then he turned to the dog. "What do you think, Mickey? Okay if we crash here for a while?"

Mickey just wagged his tail. Then he went outside, lifted his leg and peed on an upright post. "Mickey D says thanks. Me too."

Chapter Eight

Ray loaned me a nine-foot tri-fin board
and told me to keep the wet suit. He
dropped me off at home and I felt like
a king. Now I had my own surf gear.
I could surf whenever I wanted.
Suddenly summer didn't look so bad.

Ray would show up and we'd go
back to the Farm—Nirvana Farm—
where I started to get the hang of

catching waves, riding on my belly and then finally on my knees.

But the breakthrough happened about a week later. I was all alone at the beach. The fog was back, thick as pea soup. It was seven o'clock in the morning and I had skipped breakfast. I rode my bike to the beach, wearing my wet suit and towing my board behind me on a handmade one-wheeled trailer I'd built. I heard the waves before I saw them. It was like cannons going off. I knew I shouldn't be out there alone but I had a fire in me. Today was it.

As I paddled out to the place we called the Reef (because of a rocky reef a hundred yards from shore), I felt both scared and thrilled. It was so foggy I couldn't even see the waves until they were on top of me. I had to paddle straight through five head-high walls of glass until I was beyond the break line. Then I turned around and sat on my board.

You couldn't see the shore from here. You couldn't see the waves coming. But I could feel a set approaching. I remembered Ray's advice. Don't go for the first three waves in the set. I let them pass under me. Then I lay down and took four deep hard strokes into the cold dark water.

The wave was getting steeper. I began to drop. I pushed up and got to my feet just as I hit the bottom of the wave. I stood up and leaned left, digging in with my back foot until the board began to turn. I was riding high and fast on this amazing wall of water through an invisible world. I could hear the wave breaking right behind me. I adjusted my footing, inched forward on the board and started going even faster.

Suddenly, something snapped inside me. I felt calm, unafraid. Time stopped. I let out a loud yelp that could have been heard a mile down the coast. I leaned back a little, readjusting my weight, feeling the power of the wave and tapping into it.

The wave sectioned. It began to break ahead of me as well as behind me. I tucked down and grabbed the rail of my board as I drove straight into a four-foot hollow pocket that was in my path. Suddenly I was tubed, and it was glorious. But in the split second after I was gobbled up, sucked to the top of the wave and bashed back down over the falls, my board caught sideways between my legs.

It hurt a little. Well, it hurt a lot. When a gremmie gets overconfident, it is the job of the mother sea to put him in his place. I was rolled, spindled and mutilated, but I came up gulping for air and feeling like I was fully alive.

I was a surfer now and there was no turning back.

Chapter Nine

Ray settled in at the fish shack. He'd still drive down to the beach most days just to shoot the breeze with whoever would give him the time of day. Some days, even when the waves were good, he didn't surf. Despite all the sun he was getting, he looked a little pale.

I was in the water every day now. I didn't care if the waves were clean or mushy, choppy or smooth. I just wanted to be in the water. If I got to the beach early enough, I had it to myself, but by the middle of July, city surfers were on dawn patrol and it was getting harder to get a wave to myself.

I had graduated from the beach break and was surfing at Lawrencetown Point now. Nirvana Farm and some of my other "secret spots" just weren't breaking because of the swell's direction. It was the crowd at Lawrencetown or it was no surf at all.

Some of the guys laughed at me when I rode up on my bicycle with my board on the trailer. I guess it looked pretty lame.

One day I was unstrapping the board in the parking lot, listening to Gorbie and Genghis razzing each other. I usually tried to stay out of their way.

"Hey, Wheels," Genghis called to me.

I tried to ignore him.

"You, Longboard, where'd you get that old battleship?"

"From a friend," I said.

"I don't know why anyone would want to ride a big piece of crap like that."

I picked up my board and began walking toward the water. I had to walk past his car. My board slipped out of my hands and hit the front bumper of his car. I felt like an idiot.

"Sorry," I muttered.

Genghis laughed, shook his head and slapped Gorbie on the shoulder. Some other guys in the parking lot were laughing too.

As I paddled toward the point, I saw how crowded it was. My self-confidence was gone. I didn't feel like surfing anymore and thought maybe I should just go home. But a voice in my head said I couldn't let guys like Genghis get to me. I had as much right to be here as anyone.

A dozen surfers were competing for the waves at the point. Tara was there with a couple of her friends. The guys all had shortboards and wet suits that I could tell were bought this season. They watched me as I paddled toward them. Aside from Tara, no one looked friendly.

One advantage of riding a longboard is that you can take off farther out. You can catch the wave before it gets steep, so you can take off before shortboarders. I saw a dark hump on the horizon, and I paddled past the crowd toward it. When I was in position, I turned around and began to dig with my hands. The wave was approaching and I had good speed. I felt it under me and began to stand as the wave started to jack up.

As I began to drop, I was headed straight for the pack of surfers in front of me. They began to scatter, right and left. I was used to surfing with Ray or alone. This was crazy.

I felt the wind in my hair and I aimed for a spot between two surfers who were bailing off their boards because they thought I was about to mangle them. I stopped breathing as I slid smoothly between them and made a wide arcing turn that took me back onto the face of the wave. The path was clear now as I pulled high up onto the wall of the wave. A feeling of peace and control came over me as I slid across *my* wave. I had balance and speed as I shuffled forward a bit, taking a cool, casual stance like I'd seen the old guys do in the magazines. Ray would have been proud.

As the wave ended, I kicked out and sat there for a minute in the shallows looking down at the rocks and the seaweed flowing in the cold clear water beneath me. It felt good to be away from the crowd. I heard someone let out a hoot and saw the next pair of waves approaching. At least eight surfers were scrambling for the late takeoff position. As the wave was about to break, I saw Tara back off as other surfers had jockeyed for position in front of her. On the takeoff, two young guys bumped into each other and fell off, and then Tim and Weed both made the drop, Tim going left and Weed to the right. Both of them snapped hard turns at the bottom and jammed back to the top of the wave in true thrash-and-bash maneuvers. There were other surfers in their way, but they didn't seem to notice or care. It was every man for himself as the inside surfers scrambled to get out of the way.

As I paddled back to my takeoff spot, I saw that Genghis and Gorbie had paddled out too. They sat on their boards right in front of me. There was no way I could take off if they were in my path. They were doing this on purpose. I felt a tingle of anger inside me but decided to play it cool. Let them take a wave or two in the next set, and then I would go for the third or fourth wave.

I listened to them insulting each other, cursing and splashing water. I couldn't tell if they were serious or just goofing around. They let wave number one pass under them and I saw Tara, farther in, paddle for it and catch it. But so did two other surfers. She got stuck in the white water and had to kick out. But that put her right in the path of whoever was about to drop in on the next wave.

And that would be Genghis and Gorbie. It was a sizeable clean peak and they were sputtering at each other, shouting, "My wave! My wave!"

Gorbie was closest to the peak, and by traditional surf rules it was his wave, but Genghis played by no one's rules. Genghis dropped straight down, reached out and shoved Gorbie off his board. Then Genghis beat his chest once like a gorilla and tore across the face of the wave. He didn't notice that Tara was right in his path, frantically trying to paddle out of his way.

At the last second, Tara dove deep and let her board go. Genghis jammed high onto the wave again and slid past her, but when she surfaced I could tell he had scared her.

Gorbie had paddled back out to catch another wave, but I already had it lined up. It was my turn. I knew I'd have to turn before even making the full drop if I was to avoid Gorbie, but I figured I could do it.

I felt the wave under me. My board was tapping into all that energy. I was off, pushing myself up onto my feet. I suddenly realized I was coming up on Gorbie too quickly. Instead of trying to get out of my way, he whipped his little board around and jammed it into the steepening wall. I barely slid past him and went for the long wall cruise.

Over my shoulder, I saw him take a late, steep drop and make a bottom turn so hard I thought he'd get a nosebleed.

Within a second he was on the wall with me, dogging me to kick out.

"My wave, Fartbreath," he said.

I was still new to the game. I should have taken the hint and kicked out. It was only a wave, after all. There would always be another. Maybe I wasn't thinking with my brain. Or maybe I didn't like being called Fartbreath. I didn't give up. I didn't bail. I stayed on my path. I could see the wave was about to close out ahead of me. It was prime time to plant my back foot and kick out, but when I inched backward by one step, I slipped slightly and lost my balance. Gorbie had gone high on the wave, and he was right above me, coming down fast.

I tried to bail but it all happened too quickly. The pointed nose of Gorbie's board drove hard into my ribs. It hurt like hell. Then he was on top of me and we were both off our boards and dropping over the falls with boards, leashes and bodies tangled together.

When we came up for air, Gorbie cursed at me. "It was my wave. You should have kicked out, creep."

My side hurt and I was gulping for air. "Sorry, dude," I said. It wasn't my fault but I was shaken and scared. Gorbie paddled away. The fins from his board had sliced into the side of my board. I was shaky as I got up onto it and immediately realized I was right in the way of Genghis. He had just dropped into a long wall and was heading my way with a vengeance.

I struggled to paddle out and away from him. As he slipped by, he shouted, "Go home, Ben. And take that pig board with you."

I paddled away from the crowd of surfers, wincing from the pain in my side.

I steadied myself and started to head in to the beach. Tara saw me and paddled over.

"You okay?"

"Dinged board, a little sore in the rib cage. Could be worse."

Tara paddled beside me to shore. When we got out of the water, she said, "I think I'll wait until the egos cool out there."

"Might take a while."

Although I was still in pain, and my own ego had been battered, I was feeling better about the world in general. Tara brushed her wet hair out of her face and smiled at me. "There's a bonfire tonight down by the inlet. You gonna be there?"

"I wasn't invited."

"Don't be silly. If you want an invitation, I'm inviting you. So?"

My heart started beating faster. "Sure," I said. "I'll see you there."

Chapter Ten

I felt bad when Ray saw the big slice taken out of his board. "That board hasn't had a ding in the last thirty years," he said.

"Sorry, Ray. Can you fix it?"

"No," he said, almost angry now. "But I'll teach *you* how to fix it. Right here. Right now."

So I had my first lesson in surf-board repair. There was sanding, cutting fiberglass cloth, mixing resin and adding catalyst. Some of the resin hardened on my hands, and that felt weird. Then I had to sand the surface again for almost half an hour.

"I'm not going to surf in a crowd anymore. That's how this happened. Surfing in a pack sucks."

"Yes, it does," Ray said. "But it's a necessary evil sometimes. And you need to confront that demon too, warrior style. But without violence."

"What?"

"It's a Zen thing, more or less. What was it you didn't like about the crowd?"

"I don't know. I didn't feel free to surf like I wanted to."

"That's where the warrior part comes in. You accept the circumstances and you fight the negative part within you. You don't have to get agro for waves or let anyone run into you, but you fight the negativity."

"How do you do that?"

Ray smiled. "You use your mind, dingo. When else is it difficult for you to surf?"

"When the waves are big."

"What are you feeling?"

"I don't know. Fear, I guess."

"It's natural. Now, you probably think I'm going to say that a wave warrior would fight the fear within him."

"Sounds logical."

"But that's not it. A wave warrior embraces the fear, knows why it is there and respects both the fear and the wave. So you look for a way to work with the fear, to turn it into something useful. And you'll be a better surfer."

"But I'm not sure I get it."

"You will. Find your center. Find your strength. Listen to the fear but don't let it control you. Instead, learn from it."

I was done sanding. "You going in the water?" I asked.

"Nah," Ray said. "I have to go to Halifax. I have some prescriptions I have to get filled. Maybe email back home and let 'em know I'm okay."

"There's a bonfire at the inlet tonight, just up from where you're staying. Drop by."

"Maybe," Ray said. "Now take better care of that board. It has a history, you know."

"I will."

I don't know what I was expecting at the bonfire. I hitchhiked there and saw a bunch of the city surfers drinking beer and smoking weed. The fire was raging. Genghis and Tim were arguing about something. I found Tara talking with some girls, and she introduced me.

"I saw you get nailed by Gorbie today," a girl named Wendy said. "You get hurt?"

"Only my pride," I said. "And my board."

"I hear there's a tropical storm off Bermuda," Tara said. "Could be waves here by Thursday."

"Don't know if I'm ready for that," I said before I realized how I'd sound.

"I am," Wendy said. "I can't wait."

"Wendy's going to be in the contest this year," Tara said. "And so am I. Surfing a real tropical swell would put us in good shape."

"Ben, you should surf in the juniors—it's sixteen and under," Wendy said.

I shuffled my feet and looked down. "Don't know if I'm ready for that either," I said.

Just my luck that Gorbie was walking up behind me right then and heard it. He'd been drinking. "Ben, man, you gotta learn not to drop in on a brother." His voice was decidedly non-brotherly.

"Sorry, I thought I had the wave all alone."

"I dropped in deep. Would have made it if you hadn't gotten in my way."

"Like I said, sorry."

"Next time, dude, your ass is grass. You better stay with the knee slappers in the shore break and stay away from the point."

Tara looked embarrassed. "It wasn't your fault," she said after Gorbie walked off.

"Here, have a beer," Wendy said. I guess she felt sorry for me too.

I wasn't a drinker. But I had this feeling I should accept it. So I did. I slugged it back and was standing with the empty in my hand when Ray walked up.

"Easy on that stuff, soldier. Been there, done that and have the T-shirt and the scars to prove it."

"Hey, Ray. This is Tara and Wendy."

Ray said hi to them, and then he stared into the blazing fire. "God, this brings back memories," he said. Then he walked off a few paces into the darkness. When he turned back toward me, I had the bizarre impression he'd been crying. I think he was about to say something to me, something important. But there were shouts.

Genghis slapped Gorbie on the head. They did this all the time. I used to think it was just playing around, but the game escalated quickly. They'd both been drinking quite a bit. Gorbie retaliated by pushing Genghis's arm up behind his back. But Genghis got out of the hold and tripped Gorbie, who rolled quickly to one side, grabbed his enemy's legs and pulled him down—right into the fire.

I don't know how Ray did it, but it was like he had seen each move of this stupid fight in advance and knew exactly what was about to happen. Genghis was falling into the fire all right, but as he neared the flames, Ray was there, reaching out with his powerful arm, grabbing him and pulling him back. Everyone froze.

Ray sat Genghis down by Gorbie on the ground. You could see that his clothes had been charred and you could smell that his hair had been singed. But he was all right. Ray said nothing to them. He walked slowly past me, looking disgusted. "This does bring back old times. And I keep forgetting that some of those old times weren't that great."

Chapter Eleven

The tropical storm stalled off the coast
and the waves came rolling in. On shore
it was warm and sunny and the water
was even warm enough to surf without
boots or gloves. That's something rare
around here.

At seven on Thursday morning, I rode
my bike with my board to the beach and
found Tara standing on the dune, looking at

the lines of six- to seven-foot waves rolling in at the Reef. Cars were pulling into the parking lot, and I knew it would be completely mobbed within an hour.

"You want to try surfing some place totally different?" I asked her as I walked up from behind.

"But this looks so perfect."

"Yeah, but look." I pointed to an SUV with seven boards on top.

"So you're willing to share your secret spot with me?" she said, smiling.

"If you promise not to tell anyone. Besides, you've been there before. I saw you on the headland."

"Let's go."

Fortunately, Tara had her father's station wagon and I could put my bike in the back. I strapped my board on top of hers and we headed east.

Ray was already in the water at the Farm when we arrived. Mickey D greeted us and walked us out to the point.

As we paddled out, the tide was low enough that some big boulders were exposed as the wave sucked out on takeoff. I watched Ray make a drop and carve a killer bottom turn around a seaweed-covered rock and then arc high up onto an overhead wall of water. He made it look like it was the easiest thing in the world.

We were paddling in deep water and moving quite fast. "We're in a rip," I told Tara. "There's one on either side of the break."

"Is that dangerous?"

"Could be," I said. "But right now it's helping us get to where we want to go."

"Yeah, but if you wipe out and snap your leash?"

"You'll get sucked out to sea."

"Keep an eye on me, okay?" she said. "This place is kinda spooky."

"We'll keep an eye on each other," I told her.

We paddled across the rip now, still feeling its seaward tug. On a surfboard, it wasn't a big deal. For swimmers it would be another story. The only way out of a rip is to swim across it, never against it. People who didn't understand this basic fact of ocean life had died on this shore.

A set of six waves was headed our way as we reached the takeoff point. Ray nodded and smiled when he saw us but didn't say a word. The way he caught the next wave and pushed himself up on the steep drop showed that he was a master surfer. I turned my board to face the shore and caught the one right behind him. Three deep strokes and I was in.

And then I saw the rock, exposed in front of me. I tried to stop but it was too late. I was already making the drop. As I stood, I began to carve hard with my left foot on the tail. The board began to turn. I hadn't meant to go right, into the collapsing wall of the wave, but I had no choice.

I felt my fin nick the big boulder as I slid past it. Close call. I was sliding across a large, steep wave and headed into a small canyon of water. The waves were so powerful that they were jacking up and throwing out, creating a tube.

For the first time in my life I was standing up and truly inside the wave. As the wave hit the shallow rocks beneath, it became hollow and there was water to my right, to my left and above me. I screamed. This was amazing.

But instead of heading away from the collapsing part of the wave, I was headed into it. And in a split second I was swallowed by it. I wiped out hard, as the wave hit me first in the head, knocking me off the board and tossing me under, then pulling me back up the wall and slamming me down hard in a big pummeling mass of white water. Ouch.

When I came up for air, my board was nearby and I was smiling so hard I thought my face would crack. I paddled out of the impact zone, back into the helpful rip, and let it drag me back out to the break. Tara was sitting there on her board and so was Ray.

"I thought, if you lived, I might try one too," Tara said.

"Dude," Ray admonished me with a grin, "you're supposed to go away from the break, not into the throat of a monster like that."

I shrugged. "Who put the rock at the bottom of the wave anyway?"

"Glaciers," Ray said. "Long time ago, one of them thought it would be a dynamite joke to plant a boulder like that in the middle of the best surf break on the east coast of North America. They waited a long time, but they finally got some yuks out of it. Nice wipeout. A classic."

Tara was giggling as she started to paddle for her own wave. She positioned herself so that she'd be able to go left and avoid the rock entirely. She took off as if in a dream, made the most graceful drop and carved hard at the bottom with her long hair flying in the bright summer air.

"You gonna marry her?" Ray joked.

"What?"

"She's beautiful, smart and she surfs like a goddess. What more could a man want?"

Tara was riding high on the wave, but it looked like it was about to section. I was thinking about those other rocks I'd seen as we'd paddled out. She'd have to keep her wits about her the whole length of the ride.

I decided to paddle for the next wave and be nearby in case she got into trouble. As the wall jacked up behind me, I suddenly felt something in the back of my brain. It was fear, pure and simple. As things went into slow motion, I felt the fear of another wipeout, the fear of getting smacked in the nose with my board. It caught me off guard and I almost lost it, but I looked back at Ray and he was staring at me, two thumbs in the air. I decided not to fight the fear but recognize it and use it.

I got cautiously to my feet. I made sure I had perfect balance before making my bottom turn, and there I was, going left into the deep bay with a perfect over-head wall of blue-green water ahead of me. The ride was steep and fast and I carved a few turns—slow and steady like a guy on a longboard should.

And when I kicked out at the end of the wave, Tara was there in the water, climbing back onto her board. We were out of the impact zone and in the rip, drifting back out to sea, getting a nearly free ride back to the break.

We surfed until our arms were noodled and our feet were pruned. Tara and I were saltwater stoked and soggy and had to lie down on the smooth warm stones of the shoreline before we could find the energy to walk back to the car.

Ray sat there on the stones with Mickey D, looking back out to sea. "I needed that," he said. "Guess that was why I drove across the continent. Kind of puts a nice touch to the end of the story."

What story? I wanted to ask, but Ray had already picked up his board and was walking back to his van. As he was walking away, Tara rolled toward me and took my face in her hands. She kissed me hard on the mouth, and then I kissed her back. She tasted like salt, and I guess I did too.

Chapter Twelve

There were two more good days of tropical storm waves. I surfed Nirvana Farm and another spot farther down the shore with Tara. It was a place called the Wreck because a steamship had run aground there in the 1930s. You could still see chunks of the hull on the shore, and part of it was beneath us where we surfed in the clear dark water. The waves were perfect A-frames with a right and a left ride from the peak. Tara and I could both take off at the same time and turn in opposite directions, sliding smoothly down away from the peak.

We were still sitting near the break at the Wreck when Tara said, "You know, you should surf in the contest this weekend."

I had decided to steer clear. "No way. I'd get chewed up."

"Not necessarily. You'd have three options. Go in the junior men's division. Or go in the longboard. Or go in both. Hey, what do you have to lose?"

"It's not my scene. I'm a loner, remember?"

"Well," she said, paddling for an upcoming wave, "I've entered the women's category. And there's some stiff competition. I don't expect to win. I just want to do it."

The wave picked her up then, and she made an amazing drop. She did a hard bottom turn, jammed it to the top of the wave and pulled a brief but heroic floater before she dropped again with full control. If it was the last heat in a contest, she'd have cleaned up.

I hadn't seen Ray for a couple of days, which felt odd. I assumed that he had driven down the coast with his dog to catch some of the remaining tropical storm waves at some truly remote locations. But that evening I rode my bike over to my grandfather's old fish shack to see if he had returned and to swap some stories with the big kahuna.

I knocked.

"C'mon in," he said.

I went in and Mickey D greeted me with the usual wagging tail. Ray was sitting in a stuffed chair reading a book called *An Avalanche of Ocean*. He didn't look so good.

"You all right?" I asked.

"Yes," he answered assertively, "the universe is unfolding as it should. Ever hear that one before?"

"No, I don't know that much about the universe. Spent my whole life here on the Eastern Shore."

"And a lucky gremlin you are."

"You find your own secret point break or what? Didn't see you at the Farm."

Ray put his book down. He looked old and tired. "I was feeling a bit wasted. Had to lay low for a few days. Gettin' old, I guess."

"Anything I can do?" I asked.

"Yep," he said. "Surf in the contest Saturday. Just to see what it feels like."

"Did Tara tell you to say that?"

"Nope. Women don't tell me what to do. I saw the posters at the beach, figured it'd do you good. Take you to the next level."

"I didn't think you liked the idea of surfing competitions." I spat the final word out.

"It's good mental discipline," Ray said. "Hell, I don't want you to become a full-fledged professional poster boy for wet suits. I just want you to confront the things that scare you."

"I didn't say the contest scared me."

"Then what do you have to lose?"

"Thirty bucks. That's what it costs to enter."

Ray cleared his throat, pulled out his wallet and put a twenty and a ten into my paw. "Now you don't have an excuse."

Seemed like I was being shoved up against a wall. "You gonna be there to coach me?"

"Sure, I'll be there."

I was scared. Surfing alone with no audience was one thing. Surfing in a contest with a couple of hundred people watching was something else. But I decided to do it. I registered at eight in the morning and watched the parking lot fill up with rowdy, stoked surfers. The air was cold, the wind was onshore and the waves looked mean and choppy. They were not perfect conditions by a long shot. Whoever could surf bumpy, close-out waves was going to win.

Tara showed up late and just barely registered in time. She was up against at least twenty other girls and women.

I stood around in my wet suit for over an hour until my first heat—the juniors—came up. Just my luck, I was up against Genghis, Gorbie and Weed. It couldn't get much worse. And I was the only junior on a longboard. The air horn sounded and we ran for the water. I was wasted and breathing hard by the time I'd paddled through the incoming waves. Gorbie gave me a threatening grin and went for the first wave headed our way. I didn't even try. He took a quick, late takeoff, punched off the bottom and back up to the nasty lip of the wave. He smacked it hard intentionally and sent a rooster tail of spray way into the air. You could hear people on the beach cheering loudly.

Genghis was on the next wave and was equally aggressive. Weed hung back and took a fairly easy wave, made a good drop and cranked around a couple of sections. Me, I wanted to go home. What an idiot I was to think I could do this.

I was alone when the next bumpy set arrived. I should have let the first two or three waves pass and go for the next one. But I was antsy, so I made a bad decision and went for the first wave. I caught it, but it began to break right away. It was a big messy wave with hardly any wall to it. I dropped and tried to turn, but the board stalled. I had barely stood up and was trying to claw at the water to get some more speed. But it was too late.

A big lumpy pile of white water slammed down on me, knocking me from the board and pummeling me. The water was surprisingly cold today. When I popped up, I could see I was right in front of Weed, who was trying to paddle back out. I grabbed my leash but not before the next wave had picked up my board and driven it toward him. Weed had to dive to get out of the way. He was cursing me as we untangled our leashes.

After that, winded and skittish, I found myself being dragged down the beach by the cross current as I tried to paddle back out against a seemingly nonstop onslaught of heavy waves.

By the time I was back in the contest zone, I had two minutes left.

You needed at least four waves to complete a heat. I had caught only one—and a shoddy one at that. My heart was thumping hard, and I felt like crap.

I waited for a wave that no one else was going for and I dug in deep. It caught me almost like the one before, but I took off on an angle this time, using the advantage of the long-board to race across the wave without having to make a bottom turn. I had a wind-chopped, head-high wall to work with and got some distance before it sectioned. I grabbed a rail and squatted low and made it past the white water and back up onto the wall as it steepened in the shore break. I tucked in low again and let this big mass of shore break— more sand than water—curl its vicious fist above me. When it came down, it came down like a steel pipe on the back of my neck.

I ended up right on the beach, in a sprawl, with a second shore-break killer wave pounding me into the sand. I felt dizzy and wobbly as a third wave smacked me off my feet when I tried to retrieve my shore-battered board.

Then the air horn blew. And I looked up to see at least a hundred people on the beach in front of me. They were looking right at me. And they were laughing.

Chapter Thirteen

Tara was walking toward me. I didn't want her feeling sorry for me. I wanted to get the hell out of there. She'd do better if she wasn't hanging out with a real loser.

I almost got away, but Ray pulled up just as I was about to walk home with my board and my wounded pride tucked under my arm. He got out of his van and put himself in my path. His skin was pale. He was sweating even though it was cool.

"Humbling, isn't it?" He could read me like a book.

"No philosophy lesson today, okay?" I was feeling mean and didn't want to have to hear any of his little speeches.

"Thought you were going into the longboard division too."

"I had enough for one day."

"Hell, man. If you're losing, be the best at it. Go for broke. Be the best at losing. I take it things didn't go well in the juniors."

"Gee, Ray, you're, like, psychic. You should have your own TV show." I had never been this rude to him before. I just couldn't help myself.

"You could probably use that edginess. Make it work for you."

"I'm done with contests, Ray. I wish you hadn't talked me into it. It sucks all the fun out of surfing."

"Sorry about that," he said seriously. "Some things do suck all the fun out of anything."

"How would you know?" I asked, wanting to be out of this conversation.

"I'll tell you one thing that kind of takes the joy away. Dying, Ben. That's the chip on my shoulder. I'm dying. I've known it for a while, and the thought does get in my way sometimes. Like on a good day back there with you at Nirvana Farm. I kept thinking, I may never get to experience this again."

"What are you talking about?"

Ray had to lean against his van. Mickey D poked his head out the window and licked him on the cheek. "I came here to die, Ben. I've been fighting cancer for about three years, but it's been winning. I was feeling better when I came here but knew it couldn't last."

"You're making this up."

"Hey, I wish I was. I didn't write this script. I'd pencil in a happy ending, but maybe this is as happy as it gets. I was at the hospital this morning. Reviewed the whole thing with the cancer doctors here. They figure I should have been dead months ago. So it could be any time now."

I felt light-headed. "Ray, I'm sorry."

"Don't be sorry. I got to live one hell of a life. No big complaints." He paused. "I could have stayed home in California and watched all my buddies feeling sorry for me. Hell, they'd even let me steal their waves because they knew I only had a few more rides before lights out. But I had this vision in my head—being on the road with Mickey D and coming here. I'd always wanted to come to Nova Scotia. So I decided to come here to surf and then…well, you know."

My throat was tight and I couldn't talk.

"What can I do to help?" I finally said. The dog was licking his face again. For the first time, I could see it in him. I could see death catching up with him. I could see it in his eyes.

"Surf, Benjamin. Go in front of all those people and surf in the longboard heat. Surf like a god or surf like a gremlin, but just go do it. And I'll watch."

It was the last thing I wanted to do.

"What if I suck?"

"If you're gonna lose, lose big-time. Have some fun with it. Show 'em all you can take it."

Twenty minutes later, I was paddling back out into those gnarly, bumpy brown waves. The chop was worse.

The waves were worse. My competitors were all older guys who knew how to handle the conditions. They were good. They made it across difficult sections, they had some longboard moves—walking to the nose, and one guy could even do a spinner.

All I could do was make the drop, get a few feet across a wall and then get walloped by the dirty lip of the thick wave. I took off on six waves. I got creamed by every one. But I just kept paddling back out for the punishment until my twenty minutes in hell were over.

When the horn sounded and I got out of the water, people started cheering. They had loved the wipeouts. Spectators always do.

Ray was smiling at me as Tara ran up and put her arms around me. "You were amazing," she said.

"I did terrible."

"Yeah, but you kept paddling back out and didn't seem to care that the waves were eating you up."

"How'd you do in your heat?" I asked.

"I lost," she said. "But I didn't lose as well as you."

Ray joined us and we waited for the scoring. I came in dead last in my heat.

"Warrior mentality," Ray said. "Congratulations."

Chapter Fourteen

Ray only let me visit him once in the hospital, and it wasn't easy. I was still hurting from the death of my grandfather. And now this.

"I bet there are some kind of waves wherever it is I'm going," Ray said the one time I did see him. "May not be the Atlantic or Pacific, but I hope they're blue and fast and full of light.

Think of me as a cosmic surfer when I die."

He was still making a joke out of it. And I was mad at him. It didn't seem fair and it didn't seem at all right. Ray had taught me a lot of good stuff and now he was leaving. I almost wished that he had never shown up. Never taught me what I needed to know about surfing. "I still don't get it," I said with some bitterness in my voice. "Why did you come here to Nova Scotia if you knew you were in such bad shape?"

He took a deep breath and looked straight at me. "I wanted the feeling of a fresh start. I wanted it to be like back at the beginning." He paused and looked at the ceiling. "And I guess I wanted to meet a kid just like you. Someone young and uncertain but with a great future ahead of him."

"What makes you think I have a great future?"

His manner changed, and he was back to the old Ray I knew. "Hey, dinghead, when the big kahuna tells you about your future, you listen up. The man don't lie."

I wanted to tell Ray I didn't have a clue about what I was going to do with my life, but I kept my mouth shut. The room felt awfully hot.

"You gotta take care of Mickey D for me," Ray said.

I nodded. I couldn't speak. I was about to cry. Mentioning Mickey D made every-thing suddenly seem real. He really was going to die if he was giving me his dog.

Some of Ray's old friends and girl-friends from California started showing up midweek. I met a few of them at the beach. They knew who I was because I had Mickey D with me. It was flat all week. Not a ripple in the ocean. It was as if the sea knew about Ray.

Ray died on a Saturday, one week after the contest. On Tuesday, a taxi arrived at the beach right after sunrise, and the driver, holding a golden urn, got out and looked nervous. Tara and I were already there in our wet suits. So were about twenty of Ray's friends from California. A big Hawaiian-looking guy named Carlos took the urn with Ray's ashes from the driver and carried it down to the water's edge.

Then Carlos picked up his twelve-foot board, set Ray's urn on it and began to paddle out to sea. We all followed him. The water was like glass. The gulls dipped and swooped above, and you could see the kelp waving back and forth in the clear water below.

We paddled about a mile out to sea, near Shut-In Island. I'd never been this far from shore on my board before, and I felt excited, spooked and sad, all at the same time. I could tell that Tara was a little scared, but she was trying not to show it. Carlos stopped paddling and we all formed a circle. Four seals popped up close to us and stared with those big sad eyes. And from high above, you could hear the beating wings of a pair of Canada geese flying over. Even higher up you could see the vapor trails of American jets on their way to Europe.

Carlos held up the urn, and each surfer in turn said something to Ray. Some said something funny, some said something serious. I knew that everyone said something that was true. When it was my turn, all I could say was "Thanks, Ray. Thanks for teaching me to surf."

Then Carlos poured Ray's ashes onto the surface of the sea and there was silence. After about ten minutes we all paddled back to shore.

By mid-afternoon, a funny thing happened. The sky became overcast and yet there was still not a breath of wind.

Waves began rolling in. Sleek four- to six-foot waves came in sets of seven. There was a lull of nearly five minutes between each set.

"I've never seen anything like this before," Tara said. We were sitting on the beach, eating vegetarian sandwiches that one of the Californians had made for everyone.

"It's a long time between sets," I said. "Ray told me that means the waves are coming from really far away."

Carlos was sitting nearby and he smiled. "Yeah, bro. Long way. Like from off the coast of Africa or something. Time to surf, my friend. Looks like Ray pulled some strings somewhere."

And so we all got back into our wet suits and paddled out to the Reef. The waves were fast and smooth, and the glassy walls allowed us to carve up and down. I had never seen such graceful surfing before. Then Tara and I took off on a wave together. I took off closer to the peak but told her to stay on. We both arced high up onto the wall and tracked in perfect unison, and I felt like we had bonded in a way I thought was impossible.

The waves lasted for two hours and then, as mysteriously as they had begun, they stopped. It was as if someone had just thrown a switch.

"Someone forget to put money in the machine?" Carlos joked. But we all knew that it had something to do with Ray. Somehow.

By the time we paddled in, the city surfers started arriving. They'd all been to the beach earlier that day and seen that it was flat. Then someone phoned in the news of the freak swell. But now it was gone. I'm not sure who said it. I just know that it wasn't me. I was petting Mickey D, scratching him behind the ears, when I heard the words: "Man, you guys should have been here an hour ago. You missed it."

Chapter Fifteen

After that the summer kind of evaporated. I felt haunted by the loss of Ray. I sat in my grandfather's fish shack with Ray's old boards and his photos and thought about a lot of things: surfing, school coming up in the fall, Tara, me. Ray's old van sat rusting out front. I slept at the shack sometimes and once invited Tara to stay the night with me.

I guess I tried to push things a little too far and she stopped me. I got the point so I apologized to her. She still spent the night, but we had a hard time talking to each other in the morning.

Through August and September, the hurricane waves never made it to these shores. I was back in school. It felt like a door had shut forever on some happy chapter of my life. I got in the ocean when I could and paddled a lot, but I can't say I had much in the way of exciting surf.

But then in early October, a tropical storm off Florida turned into a monster hurricane that tracked north and stalled offshore. The sea went wild with monster brown foamy waves pounding the coastline. There were traffic jams at the beach as people from Halifax and Dartmouth drove out just to look at the storm waves.

A couple of guys tried to paddle out only to be slammed back in the shore break.

It was an out-of-control ocean and the waves were not to be surfed. I tried to tell one of them it was stupid to surf in these conditions. He said it was none of my business. I could see that he was really cold from just a few minutes in the water. That seemed odd, so I walked down and stuck my hand in the ocean. It was bloody cold.

The storm had moved north, just below Newfoundland, and kept churning big killer waves our way. And it had created an upwelling that made the water icy cold. The water was so uninviting I wanted to give up on surfing. But there was a kind of fever in the air and surfers arrived in the parking lot each morning, waiting for the ocean to clean up, waiting for a chance to surf double-overhead waves.

And then it happened. The wind went offshore. The waves were steep and hollow. All the usual places were still unsurfable, closing out with killer waves. But on the west side of the

Lawrencetown headland, right where the river emptied into the ocean, was a clean surfable peak. A lot of guys were standing on the headland, looking down at the wave in awe. It was huge—a fast, hollow, salt-spray-spitting, grayish green wall of water that looked big enough to eat a man alive. But was it makeable?

I watched Gorbie and Genghis putting on their wet suits, heard them arguing and watched as they ran down the steep side of the headland to surf the peak. I wanted to say something to them. I wanted to remind them that it was near low tide. The river was emptying into the sea. A powerful current—not a rip, but a powerful river current—was sweeping straight out to sea, right alongside the break. If someone lost a board, they'd be swept to their doom.

All I got out was "Guys…the river…"

It was Genghis who spit on the ground as he ran past, and all he said to me was "Piss on it," which I assumed meant he didn't want my advice.

Everyone watched as they entered the water below and paddled that same river current out toward the break. It looked almost too easy. Some of the other surfers started unstrapping their boards to follow. I knew how dangerous that river was. Swimmers had drowned here before.

Tara arrived then and looked at me. "You're not going out there, are you?" She touched my arm and looked in my eyes. She still cared about me.

"Not today," I said. "I'm dying to surf. But this is all wrong." I pointed to the foam from the colossal breaking waves that was being swept out to sea in the current.

Genghis made a heroic takeoff and almost made the drop before a big mushroom cloud of exploding white water knocked him off his board. He came up sputtering.

We could see that his board had been broken clean in two. He was in close to the rocks in the shallows. All he had to do was drag himself out without getting knocked down and he'd be okay. There was a crowd of surfers and non-surfers on the headland, and they cheered as if it had all been a performance.

Next, Gorbie executed an amazing late takeoff, made the drop down a twelve-foot wall and made a bottom turn, heading away from the peak. It looked like something out of a magazine. He tracked across the wave, dragging his hand and barely keeping his balance. I was sure he was going to make it.

Then the wave sectioned and it was like the fist of God came down on his head. Hard.

Gorbie was down. Wisely, he dove deep.

His board surfaced first—very close to shore. But no Gorbie.

"His leash snapped," I heard someone yell. "He's screwed."

I walked closer to the edge of the headland. Gorbie's board was banging around on the rocks. I studied the churning white water farther out.

That's when somebody saw him. And pointed. Gorbie had tried to swim out of the impact zone and found himself in the river current. He was savvy, though. He was trying to swim across it, not against it. The only problem was that he kept getting beaten back by incoming waves that were smacking him over and over. Gorbie was at the mercy of the waves pushing in and the current pulling him straight out to sea. He wouldn't be able to get out to deeper water and he wouldn't be able to get to shore.

Tara took out her cell phone and dialed 9-1-1. She understood that this was a true emergency.

"The Zodiac will never get here in time," I said. "I'm not even sure the fire-house rescue team can handle anything like this."

"So what do we do? Stand here and do nothing?"

Tara got an operator and began to explain the situation.

I saw a couple of other guys pull up their wet suits. Weed and Tim. Right, I was thinking. Two surfers who had just toked up, heading out to sea on their short-boards. No way could they be of any help.

I was staring hard at the river current, the waves and the tiny dot that was Gorbie's head as he tried to stay above water. Almost unconsciously, I started to put on my wet suit, still looking out to sea. That's when I realized there was a small window between the killer sets of waves. Twelve waves and then a short break of maybe three minutes. Enough to get myself in the river current and paddle like hell.

When Tara looked back at me, I was already running down the hill, my longboard under my arm. She yelled, but I couldn't understand her words. I didn't have to. She didn't want me to go.

As I stumbled across the boulders at the base of the hill, I saw the lull I was looking for. Now or never. I threw myself into the foamy water and began paddling like crazy. I was totally freaked at how cold the water was. This was even worse for Gorbie. If he was getting walloped over and over, he'd lose his strength pretty quickly.

I got to my knees as Ray had instructed me and knee-paddled straight into the river current and then with it, digging with deep powerful strokes. Here at water level, I couldn't see Gorbie anywhere.

I had never been this scared before. My body was shaking. From the cold or fear, I didn't know. I just kept my head down and I paddled.

When the next set of waves arrived, I saw a huge dark mass of water coming my way. I watched in terror as it grew bigger and bigger. I prayed that I could paddle over it.

I made it. Just barely.

And then there was another.

And another.

I shifted farther into the deep water and found the river current again and worked with it. Gorbie had to be out here somewhere. The current wouldn't let him be anywhere else. When I could stop paddling for the briefest break, I looked back toward the headland. The other surfers had not made it through the shore break. I saw a couple more scrambling down the hill. All shortboarders. But they were at a disadvantage. I still couldn't see Gorbie anywhere.

And then I saw Tara on the headland, waving and pointing. When I finally saw Gorbie, he was farther out than I would have thought. The river was that powerful. He was being pulled toward a rocky shoal. The waves were crashing on the shallow reef with a terrible force. It had once been called "the Graveyard" because so many ships had wrecked there. I had to get to Gorbie. Soon.

It was all about strength, pacing, breathing, paddling. I was Gorbie's only hope. And I didn't even like the guy. I was really scared. I wondered why I was out there.

That's when I heard Ray's voice. Inside my head. *You are here because you can do this*, he said.

Do what? I was thinking. What would I do if I could even get to Gorbie?

Move past the fear. Don't ignore it. Stay focused.

I could barely breathe. I realized that I had to paddle slowly. I needed to find Gorbie but I needed to conserve energy.

And I needed to quell the doubt rising within me.

I could hear sirens in the distance. Somewhere there would be rescuers with a Zodiac. But could they even get through the waves to get here?

And then I saw Gorbie. Not struggling, but floating. His head was above the water, but he had no strength left in him. He was being pulled close to the shoal now. It was only a matter of time.

Slow and steady. My breathing came back. My lungs stopped aching. A calming voice in my head now. *Work with the sea. Don't fight it.* I kept paddling.

I turned to look back at the land. I was shocked to see how far out to sea I was. But I kept paddling. And that's when I heard Gorbie's feeble cry. It wasn't a word I could make out. But it didn't matter. I realized that, even on my longboard, even if I could get him, we were not going to make it ashore. What would I do?

And then I had him. He couldn't talk. He could barely hang on. He didn't have any gloves on and his hands were blue. I got in the water and shoved him up onto my board.

It was all pretty much slow motion. A weird kind of calm determination came over me. I had this lump of a half-dead surfer on my board. There was no way I could paddle him ashore. Gorbie was trying to hang on, lying on top, and I had to climb up half on top of him, get the nose of the board up and paddle. I had to get away from the pounding white death of the shoal, of the Graveyard.

And that meant there was only one place to go. Out to sea.

The farther from shore we got, the deeper the water. Massive swells passed under us, but none were breaking. I realized that everything was out of my hands. For now, we were alive. Gorbie tried to say something about heading ashore.

"Save your breath, bro. If we head back in there, we die."

"What then?"

"We wait. We do nothing." And then I added something weird. "Warrior mode," I said. "Save our strength and wait."

The Zodiac failed to blast through the walls of incoming water. The boat swamped and, fortunately for all, the men were washed back ashore.

Forty minutes later, after I had tried to reassure a frightened and freezing Gorbie, a search-and-rescue helicopter appeared on the horizon. Within minutes it was overhead.

The props churned up the sea, and two rescue divers dropped into the water beside us. I had been amazingly calm up to that point.

But right then I was suddenly scared to death. The rescuers harnessed Gorbie first and hauled him aloft.

And then it was my turn. The second diver took a knife and cut my leash at the last second as I was being hauled up.

Inside the chopper—an old Sea King—I was more scared than ever. "Just stay calm," said the diver who had pulled me to safety.

And then I said the strangest thing.

"What about my board?"

"I'm afraid you're going to have to let that go."

The waves subsided in a couple of days. I was glad it was over. I knew it would take a while for me to want to surf again. But I knew I would. The ocean could be deadly here, but it could be kind as well. I decided to socialize with the sea on the kinder days from then on.

I had thought about the whole ordeal, and I can't say it made a lot of sense to me. In fact, I didn't like talking about it or thinking about it. But Tara brought a navigational chart to my house and spread it out on the kitchen table a couple of days after the near tragedy.

"It shows all the currents along the shore here."

"So?"

"So, given the waves and the wind direction the last few days...and the currents, my guess is that your board—Ray's old board that he gave you—would've come ashore right about there."

She pointed to a headland farther east. The Farm. Nirvana Farm.

"No way," I said.

She just shrugged.

So we went to the Farm and we searched. There was no surfboard.

But we went back the next day and hiked farther along the coastline.

On the third day we found it—dinged with a broken fin and wedged between some rocks and driftwood. But in one piece. I picked it up and carried it home.

Mickey D actually barked when he saw the board, and I got out some fiberglass and sandpaper to begin my repairs.

As the days grew colder and the winds began to howl outside, I started thinking that this board and I had a few more rides coming our way. I kept thinking that it was time I started listening to all my teachers. Not just Ray. But Tara and the Atlantic Ocean itself and even that new voice within me—my own inner voice that had grown from a whimper to a roar.

Lesley Choyce lives and surfs at Lawrencetown Beach in Nova Scotia. He is the author of two other Orca Soundings novels—*Thunderbowl* and *Refuge Cove*—and *Sudden Impact*, an Orca Currents novel.